Meet The Author

What is your favourite animal?
The horse
What is your favourite boy's name?
Alexander – my grandson's name
What is your favourite girl's name?
Nicola, Sally, Caroline – the names of my terrific daughters
What is your favourite food?
Fish with roasted vegetables
What is your favourite music?
Classical, choral, Celine Dion
What is your favourite hobby?
Reading and country walks

Meet The Illustrator – Karen Donnelly

What is your favourite animal?
Woodlice!
What is your favourite boy's name?
Laurie
What is your favourite girl's name?
Jean
What is your favourite food?
Sausages and runny eggs
What is your favourite music?
Beck
What is your favourite hobby?
Drawing and printmaking

For Nikita

Looking for Billie

by

Rosie Rushton

Illustrated by Karen Donnelly

You do not need to read this page –
just get on with the book!

JI86,257

ET.

First published in 2005 in Great Britain by
Barrington Stoke Ltd, Sandeman House, Trunk's Close,
55 High Street, Edinburgh EH1 1SR
www.barringtonstoke.co.uk

This edition based on *Looking for Billie*, published by
Barrington Stoke in 2004

ISBN 1-842993-22-4

Printed in Great Britain by Bell & Bain Ltd

Contents

Chapter 1
How it all began ...

When I was a little kid, I was good. "She's *so* good," everyone kept saying.

"Billie's such a *good* girl," Wendy told them all. Wendy is my foster mum.

"She's as good as *gold*," Steve, my foster dad, always added. This was a joke. You see, my last name is Gold. I'm Billie Gold. Or that's what everyone calls me. No-one knows what my last name really is.

But then, no-one knows much about me at all. Even I don't know much.

What I do know is that when I left Primary School and went on to the comprehensive, people stopped saying I was good.

"Billie's not the same any more," Wendy said, at least once a week.

Of course I wasn't the same. You can't be the teacher's pet any more when you go to the comprehensive. You'd have no friends.

"Billie's a teenager now just like the others," Steve told anyone who asked about me.

He was wrong, of course. I may be 13 – but just like the others? I don't think so.

"Billie's work is late, messy and not very good," my form tutor told my parents. You see, I had more important things to worry about than World War I or French verbs.

"Now Billie's gone to the comprehensive, she doesn't care about anything any more," Wendy said every Sunday to her mother on the phone.

But she was wrong. There was one thing I cared about more than anything in the world. I thought about it every day in class. I gazed at myself in the mirror to try and find out who I was. Should I write to the newspapers to ask for help?

But I never did anything about it. Not until we had our class trip to London.

And I saw her. The woman of my dreams.

The woman on the train. The woman who could be – no, had to be – my mum.

****

I think I had better tell you the whole story. I was found in a carrier bag outside the police station when I was about 3 days old. It was a bright pink carrier bag. It came from a posh shop in the High Street. I had a blue blanket tucked round me and there was a little woolly lamb in the bag with me. I've still got that funny little lamb. I keep it under my pillow.

There's something else I keep. It's a torn scrap of paper that the policeman found in the bag with me. It just says:

Please look after Billie until ...

That's all. But you see, it's very important. It's the word "until" that matters. I'm sure it must have said "*Please look after Billie until I come back to get her*". And then the name of the person who wrote the note must have been there too. They would have written, "*Love, Jane*", or "*Best wishes, Sharon*". If it hadn't been torn, I'd know the name of my mum. Or my dad. Or someone.

Don't get me wrong – I love Wendy and Steve. They're the best foster parents I've ever had. But they are not my real family. I don't belong to them – I'm with them because someone has to look after me and they get paid to do it.

The older I got, the more that bothered me. I started to feel as if I didn't know who I really was.

"You don't look like your mum, do you?" everyone said to me when I started at my new school. It's true. Wendy and Steve are small and dumpy, and I'm tall and thin. I've got bright red hair. Their hair is dull brown.

And that's not all. Wendy is very good at art, and I can't even draw or paint at all. Steve's mad about sport, and I'll do anything to get out of P.E. and games. Wendy comes from Wales, Steve comes from Scotland. And me? Who knows? I could come from anywhere.

Most days, I feel like I'm a nobody.

When people asked about my mum and dad, I told them I was a foster child. But I never told anyone about being found in a bag. I never told them why my last name was Gold. That it was the name of the ward in the hospital where the police took me when they found me.

I said that my parents had died.

Then it was my 13th birthday. Was my real mother thinking about me. Did she wish she hadn't dumped me? I thought about all the presents she would have sent me if she'd known where I was. Was November 11th even my real birthday?

"Billie, what are you thinking about?" Wendy asked me. She's a really kind person. "If you've got a problem, we're here to help. But you have to tell us what it is."

I didn't want to upset her, or make her think I didn't like her, so I just said I wasn't feeling well. She said it might be because my periods would be starting soon. Only 3 girls in my class hadn't started and it was so uncool. If they didn't come soon, I'd have to pretend.

"I expect your mum started late too," Lisa said. "But of course you'll never know."

Lisa's the only one of my mates who knows about the carrier bag and how I was found. I didn't mean to tell her. But I did. One day she was crying because her dad had left home to live with Bimbo Bev. Her mum kept taking tablets for her nerves and forgot to buy them any supper.

"You're so lucky having a mum and dad who care about you," she sniffed.

So I told her that Wendy and Steve were only foster parents and that I didn't know who I was. Just to make her feel better about her life.

"How romantic!" she said. "Just think about it. You could be the love child of someone famous."

Lisa's always making up fantastic stories. She can lie like anything when she needs to. Somehow Lisa can get away with anything. The only people she can't boss around are her parents.

That's why I'm glad I told her. That's why I'm glad it was Lisa who was with me that day.

The day that people began to see that I was not always as good as gold.

Chapter 2
What did you say?

We were going on a school trip to London and Lisa had got hungry on the train. That's how I saw this woman.

"We need to get crisps and chocolate," Lisa told me. "Miss Webber will go on and on about moons and planets and stuff at the Science Museum. It will be even more awful if we're feeling hungry."

Miss Webber is our science teacher. She forgot to book a coach to get us to London. So she and Mr Brown (who teaches P.E. and is madly in love with Miss Webber) took us by train. There were only 16 of us on the trip, so they thought they could cope. I think later on they wished they'd stayed in school.

Anyway, when we got to the buffet car, we saw this really huge woman. She was leaning on the counter with a big pile of cakes and sandwiches in front of her. She wore a purple velvet dress and every time she moved to pick up a sandwich, her boobs shook and her gold bangles jangled. She wore a turban on her head. She looked like someone out of Aladdin.

"Now tell me, dear," she said to the girl behind the counter, "does this sandwich have butter in it? Because I never eat butter. It does? Oh dear."

She tossed it aside.

"And this cake – is it sugar-free?" she asked.

Can you have sugar-free cakes?

She went on for ages, prodding and sniffing.

"I've made up my mind!" the woman said in the end. "I'll just have …"

Then her mobile phone rang – loudly. She grabbed it and clamped it to her ear.

"Hello? It's Pixie here – who are you?"

"Pixie?" said Lisa. "What kind of a name is that?"

The girl behind the counter grinned at us.

"Can I get you something?" she asked. "Don't worry about her, she'll take ages choosing. She's the same every day."

"I'll have a Mars Bar and a Twix and a Kit Kat ..." Lisa began.

Just then a voice came over the intercom.

"We shall soon be arriving in London. This train stops there."

"Oh my goodness!" The woman called Pixie grabbed a flapjack. Then she slammed a pound coin onto the counter.

"Got to go," she yelled into the phone. "We're at the station."

And she pushed past us.

"Ouch!" yelled Lisa as Pixie trod on her toe. Pixie was still shouting into her mobile.

"What am I doing?" she boomed into the phone. "What do you *think* I'm doing, you stupid man?"

She sounded cross.

"I'm doing what I've been doing for the past three years. Looking for Billie."

****

I can't quite remember what happened next. I do remember that my legs turned to jelly. I remember staring at Pixie as she pushed the door open and stepped onto the platform. I remember Miss Webber yelling at Lisa and me for going off to the buffet and not staying with the rest of them.

And I remember that Lisa grabbed my arm as Pixie strode off down the platform.

"Billie!" Lisa cried. "Did you hear what she said?"

I nodded. My mouth had gone dry and I couldn't speak.

"Well, don't just stand there!" Lisa yelled. "Go after her."

"I can't," I said. "What would I say?"

"Tell her you're Billie, of course," Lisa told me. "She said she was looking for Billie, didn't she? She could be your mum."

"She *can't* be," I said. But my mind began to race. What if she was my mum? What if fate had put us on the same train that morning?

"Right, everyone," Miss Webber said loudly. "I want you to walk in pairs to the Underground. Mr Brown will lead the way, I'll come at the end."

"Keep together now," Mr Brown cut in. "Follow me."

"Billie," Lisa hissed in my ear, as we all went through the ticket barrier, "it's now or never. Look, there's Pixie way in front."

I bit my lip. Lisa was right. Any second now Pixie would vanish and I would never see her again.

J186,257

"Miss, I need the loo," I told Miss Webber.

"Well, you'll have to wait until we get to the museum," Miss Webber said.

"I can't, Miss," I yelled, and I started to run.

"I need to go too," Lisa yelled behind me. "We'll meet you at the Underground."

I prayed that Mr Brown wouldn't follow us.

We rushed past the ticket man, who yelled at us, and ran across the station. We could only just see Pixie. She was walking towards the taxi rank.

Pixie was walking very fast. But if the laces of my trainer hadn't come undone, I'm sure we would have got to her in time. As it was we reached the taxi rank just as she was getting into a black cab and slamming the door shut behind her.

"Wait!" yelled Lisa at the top of her voice, jumping up and down and waving her arms in the air.

For one great moment, I thought Pixie had seen us waving and shouting. She turned and looked me in the face.

Then she said something to the driver, and the black cab drove off.

Just as the cab started off, Pixie pulled off her turban and shook out her hair. It was bright red. Not a soft red, not rust or ginger. It was flaming orange. Just like mine.

Chapter 3
Follow that cab!

"Come on!" Lisa grabbed my arm and pulled me towards the next taxi in the line.

"What are you doing?" I asked.

"We're going to go after her, of course," Lisa told me and she pulled open the cab door. "Get in."

"You're mad!" I yelled. "We can't just bunk off."

"Get real, Billie!" she shouted. "This is your only chance. Get in!"

Lisa pushed me into the cab and slammed the door.

"Follow *that* black taxi!" she yelled to the taxi driver. "Quick!"

"I don't know about that," said the driver.

"My mate's mum's in there," Lisa said. "They've had an awful row, and my mate here wants to say sorry."

The cab driver grunted.

"That's nice," he said. "A kid who says sorry. Doesn't happen often."

He pulled away from the kerb. My heart was beating hard.

"Lisa, you're bonkers. Miss Webber will go ballistic," I said.

"So? What matters more to you? Your whole life or Miss Webber getting cross with you?"

Lisa was right. It was just that I wasn't someone who broke the rules. But Lisa was an expert at it.

"That woman just has to be your mum," Lisa said. "Until I saw her, I thought you were the only person on the planet with hair as bright red as that."

She patted my hand.

"Just think," she said, "there's your mum looking for you and she doesn't know you're in the taxi right behind her. It's like something out of a film."

But in films something bad always happens just when you don't expect it.

And that's what was about to happen to us.

****

There was a lot of traffic and the taxi was going very slowly. We could still just see Pixie's black cab some way in front. Then the intercom in our cab crackled into life.

"Oscar three seven, can you hear me?"

The cab driver flicked a switch.

"I can hear you," he said in a bored voice.

"We've got some mad woman on the line in a panic. Have you got two kids in your cab? One with bright red hair and one with a ponytail?"

I gasped.

"They've run away from a school group. Their teacher's in an awful state. You must take them to the Science Museum at once."

"Run away, huh?" said the driver angrily. "All that talk of mums. You kids, you're all the same. Lying, bunking off ..."

"It's not a lie!" Lisa yelled. "That woman is my mate's mum."

"Oh, sure," the driver grinned. "And I'm Spiderman."

"Please," Lisa said. "You have to believe us. We have to catch up with her. Billie's whole life is on the line here."

"My job will be on the line if I don't get you two back to your teacher," he said and he sped off.

"You can't do this to us!" Lisa yelled at him.

"Yes I can," he told her.

"I said it was a crazy plan," I said to Lisa. I wanted to cry. "We're going to be in dead trouble and for what? Some woman I'm never going to see again."

"That's where you're wrong," Lisa said.

"Wrong about getting into trouble with Miss Webber? I don't think so," I told her.

"You're wrong about never seeing that Pixie woman again," Lisa went on. "I'm not the sort of person who gives up just like that. We'll find her, however long it takes."

I didn't believe a word of it. But I didn't have time to tell her so because the taxi was stopping outside the Science Museum. And there was Mr Brown, walking up and down and looking really, really angry.

Chapter 4
Teacher Trouble

"And what do you two have to say for yourselves?" Mr Brown yelled at us as we opened the taxi door.

"Sorry, sir," I said.

"Sorry? Is that all? Pay the driver at once and then I shall deal with you both."

Lisa and I looked at each other.

"How much?" I asked the driver.

"Nine pounds," he said.

"Nine pounds!" Lisa yelled. "That's a rip-off!"

Mr Brown's face went purple.

"Lisa," he snapped, "how dare you be so rude!"

"But, sir, I've only got five pounds," she told him.

"Me too," I nodded. "It will take all the money I've got."

"You should have thought about that before running off," Mr Brown yelled, as we handed over all our cash to the grumpy driver.

"What a lot of trouble you've made for a lot of people," Mr Brown said, as he marched us into the museum. "How could you have been so stupid?"

"I thought I saw someone I knew," I told him. "Someone I hadn't seen for ages."

This just made him even more cross.

"Well, fancy that," he said. "So if Miss Webber and I had spotted an old friend, do you think we would have dashed off and left you all alone?"

"No, sir," we both said together. "Sorry, sir."

I didn't get anywhere near Lisa for the rest of the day. Miss Webber made Lisa go in her group, and sent me off with Mr Brown. She got the best part of the deal. Mr Brown only smiles twice a year and his armpits smell. I had to spend the whole day filling in stupid worksheets and looking at videos about the night sky. And all the time, I was thinking about Pixie.

And her red hair.

And the fact that she was out there, somewhere in London looking for Billie.

And that maybe, the Billie she was looking for was me.

****

Chapter 5
Making Plans

"I can't believe that we were so close to finding your mum," said Lisa as we walked home from the station at teatime.

"Don't keep going on about it," I snapped. "We didn't find her and that's an end to it. Just forget it, will you?"

I knew I wasn't going to forget it, but at that moment something else was on my mind.

"Did you hear what Miss Webber said on the way home?" I asked Lisa. "She's going to report us to the Head. He'll ring Wendy and Steve and then I'll be in real trouble."

"So? You get kept in for a few days – what's the big deal?" Lisa replied. "Get a life, Billie!"

I didn't like to tell her that I'd never been kept in before. I'd been made to do the washing-up every night for a week, yes. But kept in and not allowed out with my mates? Never.

"I've got it!" Lisa cried all at once. "Why didn't I think of it before? It's simple."

"What is?" I asked.

"We get the train again tomorrow, right? That way we can sit next to her and you can tell her who you are."

"Lisa, what are you on about?" I said. "That's the most stupid plan I've ever heard."

"Why?" Lisa snapped.

"Pixie was on the train today, but she may not be on the train tomorrow, stupid," I said.

"Yes, she will be," Lisa said, with a grin. "Remember what the girl at the buffet said? She said she took ages to choose her food *every day*."

"Every day!" My mind was racing. "You're right, she did say that."

For a moment, my heart lifted. It soon sank again.

"We can't just bunk off school and catch a train," I said.

"Billie Gold, what matters more?" Lisa replied. "One day of school, or your whole life?"

What could I say?

"My life," I told her. My heart was thumping.

"Right!" Lisa grinned. "Now, listen to me. This is what you have to do."

****

I didn't sleep that night. I'm not sure if it was because I was so excited. After all, I might just meet Pixie the next day. Or was I feeling bad because of what I'd done after supper?

This is what I did. I thought I would get found out. Steve was cross that his friend hadn't phoned him to plan where to meet next day. Well, his friend couldn't phone, could he? I had unplugged every phone in the house. If the Head rang up to make a fuss about us getting lost on the trip, Steve and Wendy would be on Red Alert.

Unplugging the phone was the easy bit. Taking the money was a lot harder. I've got some cash in the bank but there was no time to get that. So I had to take it from Wendy's bag. I felt sick doing it. I put it back 3 times.

But then I said to myself that it was only a loan. When I'd found Pixie, and told Steve and Wendy the whole story, they'd understand.

All I had to do was to find Pixie and then everything would come right.

I was 13 years old. How could I be so dumb?

Chapter 6
Second-class Citizens

"Is your mobile off?" Lisa said as we waited for the train to London to start.

"No, does it matter?" I asked.

"Just think," Lisa said. "When the school phones home to say we haven't come in, Wendy will phone you, right?"

I felt sick.

"I hadn't thought of that," I said, and I switched off my phone.

"Lucky you've got me to sort you out," Lisa told me. "Hey, we're off! Come on!"

We ran along the train until we got to the buffet car.

Pixie wasn't there. But it was the same girl behind the counter.

"You know the woman who was here yesterday?" asked Lisa. "Has she been here today?"

The girl stared at her. She looked bored.

"What woman? We get hundreds of women coming here," she said.

"The one with the turban," Lisa went on. "The fussy one."

"Oh, her!" the girl grinned. "Pixie Petruso."

"Hey, Billie," Lisa said to me, "sounds like you're Italian."

Did I want to be Italian? I don't even like pasta.

"What did you say?" the girl asked.

"I just said that Petruso sounded like an Italian name," Lisa replied.

"Well, of course it is – everyone knows that," the girl said. She started to serve a tall man in a smart suit. "Don't you watch TV? She was in that Friday night play last week."

She turned away from us then. She was smiling at the tall man and giggling.

"TV?" Lisa said. "I knew it! Your mum's famous."

We waited for the tall man to march off with his sandwich and cup of coffee.

"So where is she?" Lisa asked the girl. "You said she got on the train every day."

"Well, she does," the girl nodded.

"Ace!" Lisa spun round and slapped my hand. "We've cracked it."

"You won't get to talk to her," the girl told us. "She hates to be bothered. That's why she travels first class."

"Where's that?" I asked.

"First 2 coaches," the girl said.

"Thanks!" We grinned at each other and began to push our way to the front of the train.

"And just where do you two think you are going?" The ticket man was blocking the door to the first-class coaches.

"We've got to see Pixie Petruso," Lisa began. "We've got something that belongs to her."

The ticket man shook his head.

"Not that old story again," he said. "Can't you think of a better one? Now get back to your seats," he ordered, "if you don't want to pay an extra 25 pounds to travel first class."

"But we have to see ..." Lisa started to say.

"What you have to do, Miss," he told Lisa, "is push off. Leave Miss Petruso alone. She's paid not to be bothered."

We had to go back and he followed us all the way to our seats. He made sure we stayed there, too.

"We'll just have to catch her when the train gets to London," Lisa said. "It's so exciting. She must be famous. And I expect she's very rich, too."

She looked at me with envy.

"Promise me something," she said, putting her hand on my arm.

"What?"

"When you're living in some posh house with Pixie, remember it was me that made it all happen, OK?"

"Sure," I nodded.

"You're not looking very happy about it," she said.

The funny thing was, I didn't feel very happy. I felt scared. What would happen if I found my real mum? Would I have to go and live with her? Leave Wendy and Steve? I hadn't thought about any of that.

Did I want to go and live with Pixie, even if she was my real mum? Where was she when I needed her? Did she dump me because a baby would spoil her life?

If Lisa was right, and Pixie had loads of cash, why couldn't she have found me and given me some? Been a proper mum?

By the time the train got to London, I wasn't just scared. I was angry.

Very angry indeed.

Chapter 7

It wasn't meant to be like this ...

We jumped off the train, ran down the platform and saw Pixie as she was going through the ticket gate. This time she was wearing a bright pink coat and a black turban.

We ran as fast as we could and got to her as she stopped at the taxi rank.

"Excuse me, we have to talk to you!" Lisa jumped in front of her, blocking her path.

"Not now, dears," Pixie replied. We could smell her perfume. She waved down a taxi. "I'm in a hurry."

She pulled open the door of the cab.

"No! Wait!" I could hardly speak. "It's really important."

"I'm sorry but I've no time now," Pixie replied. She didn't really look at me. She got into the cab and began shutting the door.

"Please listen," Lisa yelled as she held the door open. "We know what you're doing – looking for Billie, right?"

"Yes, dear, too right," Pixie replied. "Sometimes I think I'll be doing it for the rest of my life. Day after day, looking for Billie."

She tried to pull the door closed, but Lisa hung onto it.

"Child, let go of that door!"

Pixie's voice was angry now.

"No, I won't!" Lisa yelled. "Just listen, will you? You don't have to look for Billie any more."

"What *are* you talking about?" Pixie was getting more and more angry.

"You don't have to look any more. Here she is," Lisa told her, pointing at me. "This is your daughter."

"My daughter?" Her face went white and she put a hand to her mouth.

"Yes, me," I smiled. "I'm Billie."

"How dare you say such a thing!" Pixie yelled angrily. "You can't be my daughter!"

And that's when I went mad.

"You don't like the look of me, is that it? So you won't claim me after all?" I gulped back the tears.

"I expect you wish I'd never been born, is that it?" I said.

Pixie's face went purple.

"Excuse me," the driver said, "but are we going somewhere or not? There's people waiting behind us, you know."

"Yes, we're going right now," Pixie said, and she snatched the door away from Lisa and slammed it shut. "Papa Gino's restaurant, Covent Garden – and fast!"

"You can't just go!" Lisa yelled after her. "You can't just dump your daughter."

"Oh, yes she can!" By now I was sobbing. "She's done it before."

Pixie didn't reply. But as the taxi drove away, I saw her drop her head into her hands. She was shaking.

"How *dare* she laugh at me!" I said. I was still sobbing.

Lisa put a hand on my arm.

"She's not laughing, Billie," she said softly. "She's crying."

"Crying?" I said.

Lisa nodded. "She *must* be your mum. She's crying because she feels so bad about leaving you."

****

Chapter 8
The end of the dream?

We had no cash for a taxi so we had to catch an Underground train. It took ages and as we got closer to Covent Garden, I started to feel more and more scared.

"This is stupid," I kept saying to Lisa. "She doesn't want to know me. If she did, she wouldn't have driven off."

"That was the shock," Lisa told me. "It makes people act funny and then they wish

they hadn't. We're just giving her a bit of time, that's all."

We spotted Pixie as soon as we came into Papa Gino's restaurant. She was the sort of person who stood out in a crowd. She was sitting at a corner table, sipping a glass of wine and chatting to a tall guy with floppy black hair.

"What now?" I asked Lisa. "We can't just march up to them."

"You'll see," Lisa replied, grabbing my hand.

She dragged me over to the table.

"Remember us?" she said.

"The girls from the station," she said. "I'm sorry – I must have seemed very rude."

"It's OK," I began, but Lisa cut in.

61

"No, it's not OK!" she said, glaring at Pixie. "How could you do that?"

"Do what?" Pixie asked. She looked puzzled.

"Drive off like that," Lisa told her. "Just when we'd found you."

"Look, dear," Pixie said. "I can't talk to you right now. I'm busy with this young man. He's from a newspaper."

"Oh, well, that's good," Lisa said, "because this is an ace story."

"It is?" the guy asked.

"Sure," Lisa said with a grin. "This is Billie. She's Pixie's long-lost daughter."

"Really?" The guy looked excited. "Pixie, is this true?"

Pixie didn't reply. She just stared at me.

"Billie?" Pixie said. "Your name is Billie?"

I nodded. She had to claim me now – I've never met another girl called Billie in my whole life.

"Pixie – is this true?" the reporter asked. He was taking notes of all this.

"Of course it's not true, you stupid boy!" Pixie said crossly. "These children have just come up with some wild story."

"We're not children and it's not a story," I said in panic. "You've been looking for me. Well, here I am."

Pixie gazed at me.

"But I haven't been looking for anyone," she began.

I felt myself getting angry all over again.

"Yes, you have," I told her. "We heard what you said on the train."

Pixie was staring at me. She shook her head. Then, all at once, her eyes grew large and she put her hand over her mouth.

"Just what was it that you heard me say?" she asked, still gazing at me.

"You said you were looking for Billie," I said. Did I really want a mum who was as thick as this? "Yesterday, when you were talking on the phone."

"Oh." Pixie closed her eyes. "Looking for Billie. So that's it."

She gave a bit of a smile.

"Yes, that's it," Lisa went on. "And this is Billie, the baby you dumped in a carrier bag outside the police station."

"A carrier bag?" the reporter cried. He sounded thrilled.

"You were left in a bag?" Pixie gasped. "Oh, you poor child!"

She picked up her glass and took a gulp of wine.

"Look, let me just finish with this young man, and then I'll show you something that will sort out this silly mistake once and for all."

"Is that what you thought I was when I was born? A silly mistake?" I didn't mean to say this. It just happened.

"My dear girl," she began, but I didn't let her go on.

"So you thought you'd got rid of me for ever, did you? You minded more about being rich and famous than about keeping your baby."

By now I was really sobbing. Lisa handed me a grubby tissue. The reporter went on taking notes like mad.

"If you knew," Pixie said. "If you only knew! If I'd had a baby ..."

She took off her turban, flung it to one side and put her face in her hands.

As the turban fell to the floor, I gasped.

Lisa gasped.

Pixie's hair was cut very short.

And it was jet black.

"Your hair!" I said. "It's not red."

"Of course it's not red," she snapped.

Then she looked at my red curls.

"Oh," she said. "I get it. You saw me yesterday, didn't you? I had my red wig on."

"Your wig?" My heart sank. I could see now that she didn't look at all like me. Without the red hair, she could be just anyone.

"I was trying to get used to that awful wig," she said. "I've got to wear it for an advert for frozen pizza."

She stood up and flung on her coat.

"I'll be back in a moment," she called.

"Where are you going?" I asked. Not that I cared. She didn't matter to me any more.

"Wait a moment, and you'll find out," she said, setting off for the door. "Follow me."

We followed her down the road and turned a corner.

"Look," she said, pointing to the theatre across the road.

And that's when I understood.

In huge lights, across the top of the theatre, were the words:

LOOKING FOR BILLIE

A play in three acts

starring

PIXIE PETRUSO and MAX GRAY

"Oh no!" Lisa gasped.

My eyes filled with tears again.

"It's a play," I said dully. "And you're not my mum."

"I'm so sorry," Pixie said gently. "I would have loved nothing better than to have a daughter like you. I did have one, once. She died when she was a few hours old."

Two large tears rolled slowly down her cheeks.

I had a huge lump in my throat.

"I'm sorry," I told her. "I didn't mean to shout at you. I just wanted to know where I came from, that's all."

I gulped.

"We'll go then," I said.

"No, wait!" Pixie took my arm. "Look, tell me where you live. I'd like to send you tickets to see the play."

"I mustn't give my address to strangers," I told her.

"Very sensible, too," Pixie nodded. "Give me your school address and I'll send them to the head teacher. What's his name?"

"Mr Carter," I told her, and I gave her the address of the school.

"Right," Pixie said. "I suppose today's a day off, then?"

Lisa went pale. "What's the time?"

"1.30," Pixie said. "Why?"

"Got to go," I gasped. "We have to get back home before we're found out."

"You don't mean to say that you bunked off school to find me?" Pixie asked.

I nodded.

"Right," she said. She waved to a passing taxi. "I'll pay for you to get back to the station."

She opened the cab door.

"One more thing, Billie."

"Yes?"

"Don't worry about where you came from, my dear," she smiled. "It's where you're going that matters."

What she didn't know was that I was going to be in very deep trouble when I got home.

Chapter 9
Leave it to Lisa

"Check your phone," Lisa told me, as the train started. "Then we'll know if we've been missed."

I punched the ON button.

7 messages

The words flashed up on the screen.

Where are you? Ring me at once. Wendy.

That was the first text.

Very worried. Please ring. Wendy.

The second text.

Each text got more frantic.

The last one was really bad.

We are calling the police. Please let us know you are safe, darling. You are not in trouble. Wendy.

I started to cry. "She's calling the police," I said. Lisa went pale.

"Ring her now," she said. "Tell her we're OK. Quick."

"But where shall I say we are?" I asked. "What shall I say we've been doing?"

"Oh, give me the phone!" Lisa said crossly. She grabbed my mobile.

"Hi, is that Wendy? It's Lisa here. We're on a train from London. Yes, we're fine. We'll be home in about an hour. Pardon? Sorry, bad signal. Can't hear you. See you soon. Bye!"

She chucked the phone into my lap and grinned.

"Try again," I said. "The signal might have come back."

"You *are* dumb," she replied. "I never lost the signal. I was just giving us time to work out what we're going to tell them."

"The truth, of course," I replied.

"Sure," Lisa nodded. "But you have to do it the right way. I've got it all worked out."

"I thought you would have," I said. "But I'm fed up with your stupid plans."

There's one thing I'll say for Lisa. It's hard to upset her.

"You'll like this one," she said. "You'll like this one a lot."

Chapter 10
Mum and Me

Wendy was waiting at the station.

And standing beside her was a policewoman.

"Billie!" Wendy cried, rushing towards me as we stepped off the train, and she gave me a big hug.

I waited for her to yell at me but she didn't.

"Thank God you're safe!" she said. She hugged me hard. "I've been so scared."

She pulled away and I could see that she had been crying.

"I think, young lady," the policewoman began as we walked towards the car park, "you had better tell us what has been going on."

I was just about to start but Lisa got there first.

"We're really sorry," she said meekly, "but yesterday, Billie thought she saw her mum."

"Her mum?" Wendy said, amazed. "How could she have seen her mum? She hasn't got one."

"There was this woman, and she said she was looking for Billie, and then she took her hat off and her hair was red," I said, and then I started to cry again.

"We thought she was Billie's real mum," Lisa went on. "That's why we went back to London today. We wanted to find her."

She kicked my leg. I remembered what she'd told me to say.

"I had this dream about having a proper mum," I gulped. "Someone who would keep me forever."

Wendy stared at me.

Lisa kicked me again.

"I had this dream about having a real mum, and the woman on the train looked just like the woman in my dream." This was a lie. Lisa had told me to say that so that everyone would feel sorry for me and forget to punish me. I held my breath.

"A proper mother?" Wendy said. She sounded so upset that I began to feel bad. "And did you find this woman?"

I nodded.

"She's not my mum, though," I said. "She doesn't even have red hair. It was a wig."

"Please don't be angry, Wendy," Lisa said. "Billie's been so sad and lonely."

"Right," Wendy said. "That does it."

My heart sank. She was fed up with me.

Wendy grabbed my hand and marched us both to the car. She opened the door and told us both to get in. After that, the policewoman got into her car and drove off.

Wendy took me home and we dropped Lisa off on the way.

The moment Lisa got out of the car Wendy turned to me. "You did a stupid and selfish thing today. You do see that, don't you?" she said angrily. "I thought someone had run off with you, or that you had been hit by a car."

"Sorry," I said softly.

"Why did you do it? Why?" she asked.

"Because I want a real mum!" I yelled. "I want to know who my parents are. I want to know if I look like them. I want to belong to someone."

Wendy stopped in front of our house.

"You belong with us, Billie," she said. "We love you. You've always got a home with us."

That's when I said it.

The terrible thing.

"A foster home, you mean," I yelled. "You're not my mum. You're just a foster mum. And that is not the same!"

****

I heard Wendy crying that night.

And lots of nights after that.

I heard her talking softly on the phone. I saw her filling in forms and chatting away to Steve when they thought I was upstairs doing homework.

I knew what was happening.

They were planning to send me away.

And then one day Wendy came into my bedroom and asked me something.

I made her ask 3 times over because I thought she was just joking.

When I saw that she was dead serious, I jumped up and down and shouted, "Yes! Yes!" about 20 times.

That was 6 months ago.

I'm not Billie Gold any more.

I'm Billie Hunter. I've got a mum called Wendy and a dad called Steve. I've got a gran who lives in Scotland and at half term we went to stay with her.

She called me her lovely wee lassie and put my photo on her bedside table.

You see, Wendy had asked me whether I'd let her be my proper mum.

I said "Yes" and Wendy and Steve adopted me.

Wendy said she had wanted to ever since the first time she saw me.

Steve said they hadn't adopted me before because they thought my real mum just might turn up.

"We knew she might want to find you, Billie," he told me. "We knew you'd want your real mum and not us if you could choose."

That's where he's wrong. Things have changed.

Like Pixie said, I don't want that sort of real mum any more.

The mum I love – and the one who loves me, and supports me and makes me feel important and special – is right here.

My mum Wendy.

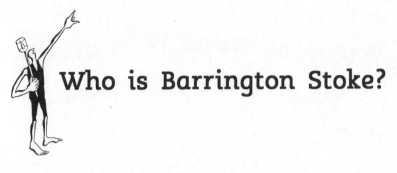

Who is Barrington Stoke?

Barrington Stoke went from place to place with his lamp in his hand. Everywhere he went, he told stories to children. Some were happy, some were sad, some were funny and some were scary.

The children always wanted more. When it got dark, they had to go home to bed. They went to look for Barrington Stoke the next day, but he had gone.

The children never forgot the stories. They told them to each other and to their children and their grandchildren. You see, good stories are magic and they can live for ever.

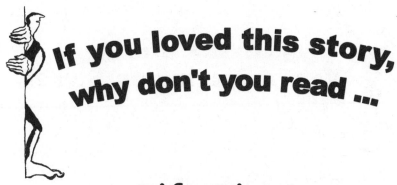

If you loved this story, why don't you read ...

Life Line

by Rosie Rushton

Have you ever told a fib because it was easier than the truth? Skid finds himself in trouble because he tells one fib too many. But how can he tell the truth about his home life?

4u2read.ok!

You can order this book directly from our website
www.barringtonstoke.co.uk

If you loved this story, why don't you read ...

Starship Rescue

by Theresa Breslin

Who can save the Outsiders from being slaves? It is up to Marc and Sasha to get a message for help to Planet Earth. But as Marc finds out, not even friends can be trusted and his task is full of danger.

4u2read.ok!